SMB, CJB, and NB –
My inspirations to make this series a reality.

www.mascotbooks.com

Frederick the Paramedic

For more information, please contact:
Mascot Books
560 Herndon Parkway #120
Herndon, VA 20170
info@mascotbooks.com

Library of Congress Control Number: 2015900494

CPSIA Code: PRT0315A
ISBN-13: 978-1-62086-832-4

Printed in the United States

Frederick
the Paramedic

written by
Chris & Nicole
Blongiewicz

illustrated by
Andy Case

Good morning, partner! Welcome to your ambulance!
Are you ready to have a great day helping people?

Fire Station

First we need to check out our ambulance.
We have to make sure the lights,
sirens, and radios work.

Do you see the lights working?
The sirens are loud and
the radios are clear!

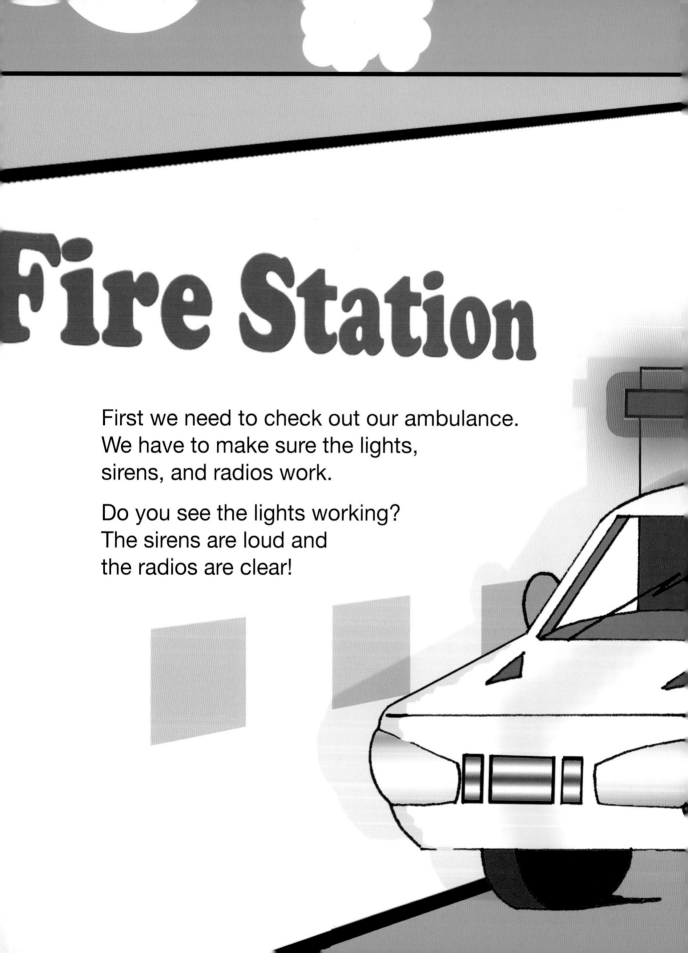

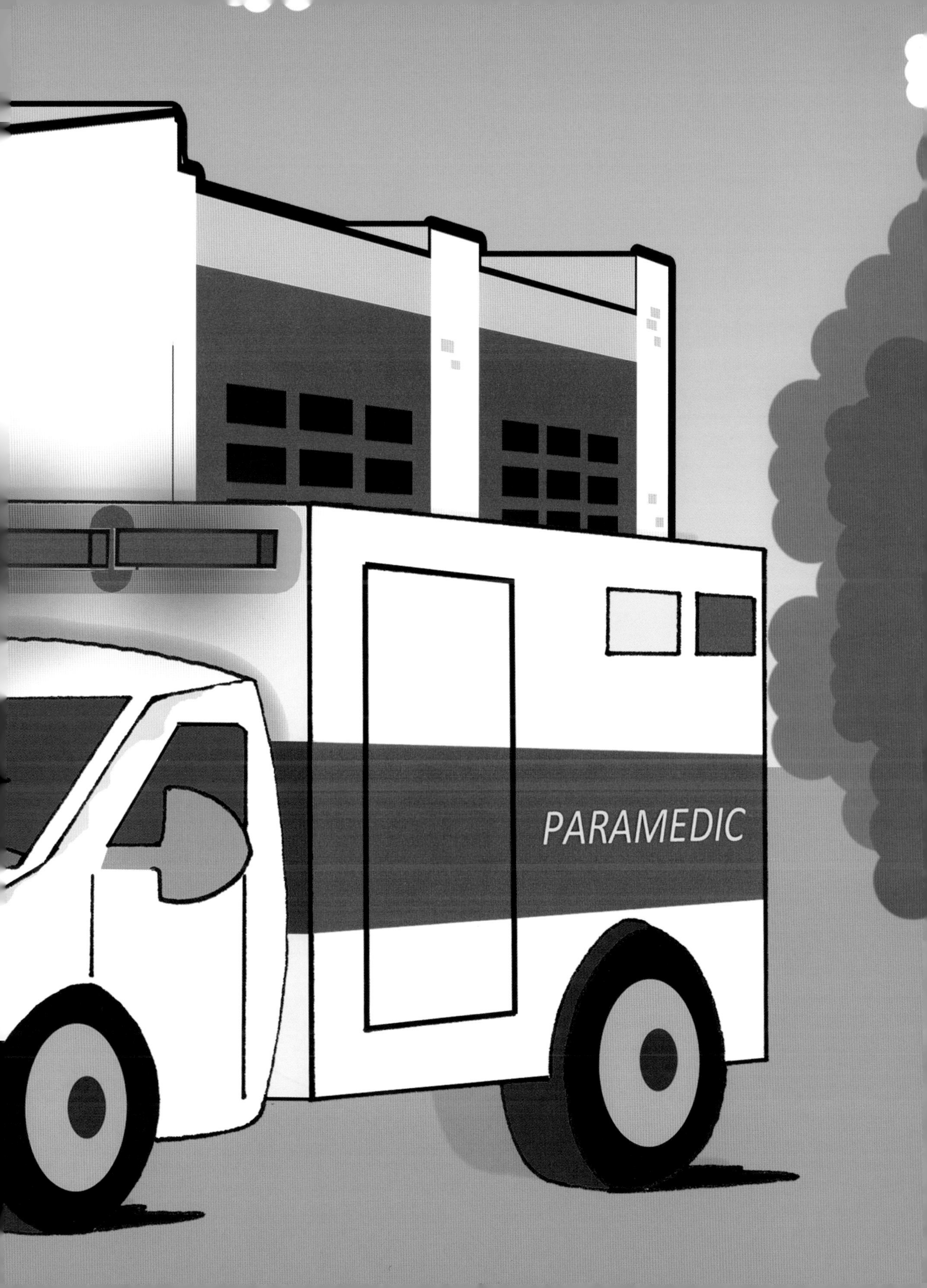
PARAMEDIC

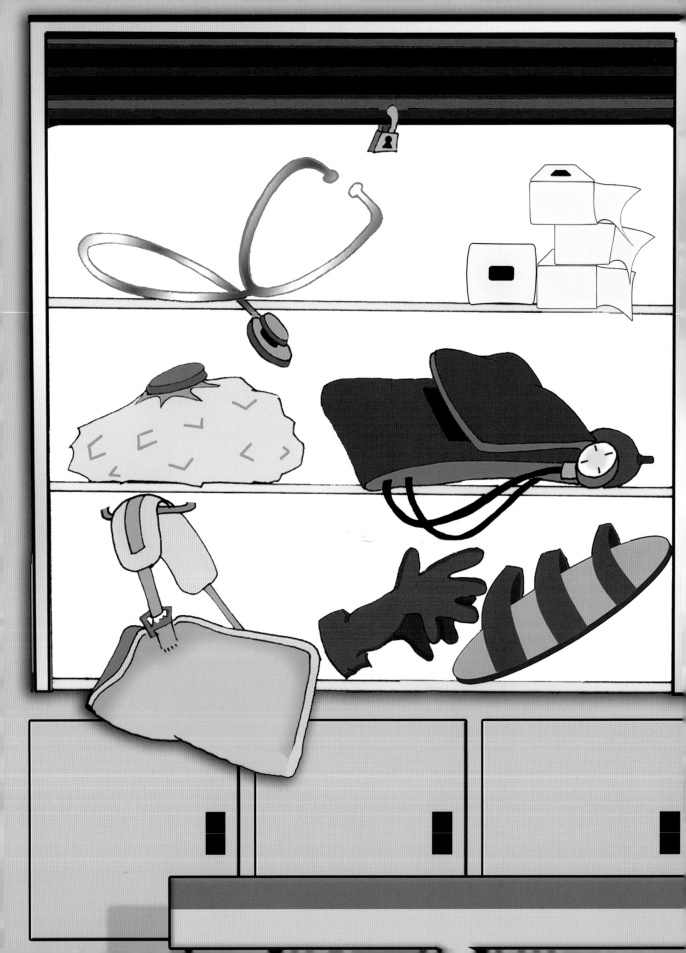

Now we have to make sure we have all of our equipment so we can help people when they have an emergency.

Can you open the cabinets and find the:

Safety gloves?

Stethoscope?

Blood pressure cuff?

Bandages?

Ice pack?

Splint?

Sling?

Super, it's all there! I'll make sure it all goes into our first aid bag so we can bring it when we need it.

Uh oh! I think there's an emergency!

"Dispatching Frederick the Paramedic! Respond to the skateboard park for an injury!"

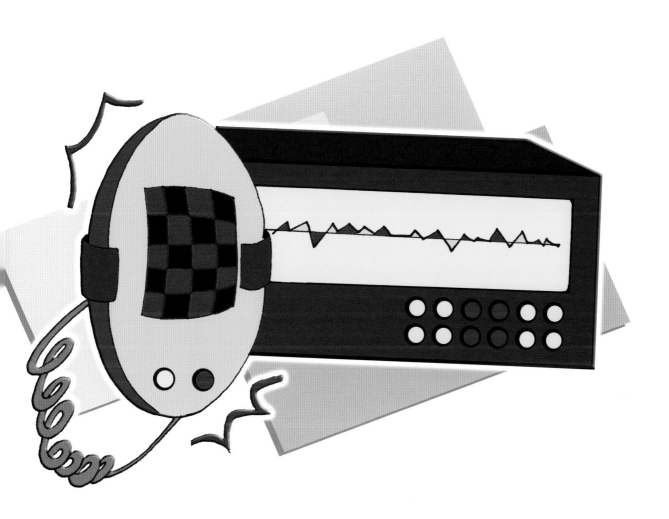

Okay! Someone needs our help.
Let's get to the skate park!

Fire Station

Let's GO!

Here we are. Look, I see a fire truck and a police car. They are here to help us. Let's go ask them what happened.

Let's ask the police officer if the scene is safe for us. Safety first!

"Hi, Officer. What happened here?"

"It seems like it was a simple accident, but the firefighters arrived on the scene first and have more to the story."

This scene should be safe for us to go into and help out.

Let's talk to the firefighters to figure out what happened. They help us in a lot more ways than putting out fires. Some of them are paramedics too!

"Hi, guys. Do you know what happened?"

The firefighter said that the skateboarder's name is Tommie, and he is twelve years old.

"He was skateboarding in the half-pipe when he fell off his skateboard. He wasn't wearing a helmet or elbow and knee pads. Right now he is complaining of some right arm pain after falling on it."

Let's go help him out!

We should introduce ourselves first.

"Hi, Tommie. I am Frederick the Paramedic, and this is my partner. We are here to help you. I heard that you were skateboarding without any safety gear, fell off your skateboard, and hurt your arm. Can we take a look at it to see if we can help you?"

Tommie said that he would appreciate our help.

"I forgot my safety gear at home. I don't usually fall, so I didn't think it was a big deal not to have it today."

Now that we have introduced ourselves and figured out what happened, we should take a look at his arm.

FIRST AID

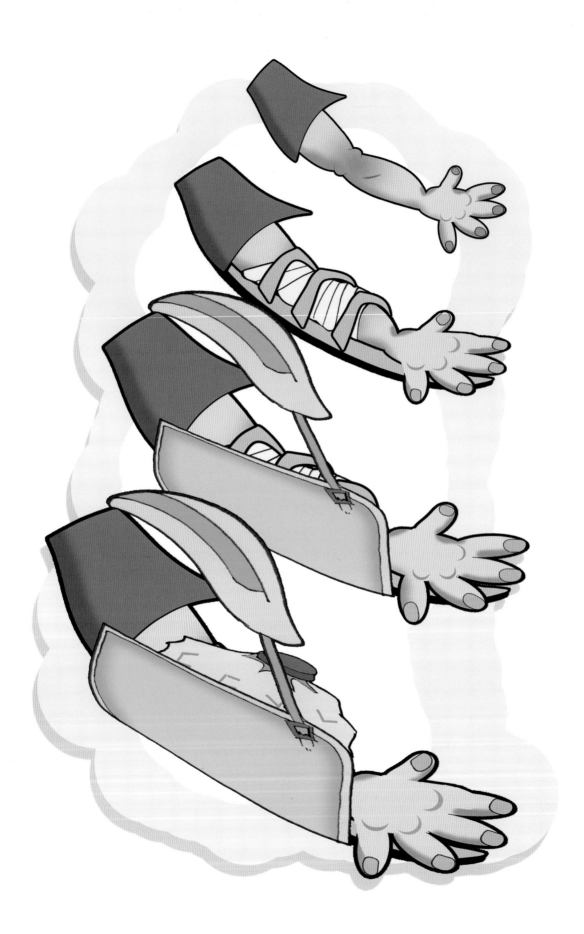

Let's take a look at Tommie's arm. Hmmm. What do you see? To me, it looks like it is red and swollen. What do you think? Do you see anything else?

Oh, there is a cut on there too. Good job, partner. I missed that!

First we need to put on our gloves to protect us and Tommie.

Now, that we have our gloves on, we need to bandage Tommie's cut. What equipment do you think we need?

That's right! We will need the bandages, a splint, and an ice pack!

Okay, let's put the bandage on his cut. That will help him feel better, and keep it clean.

Next, can you put the splint on his arm? That will limit his movement, so it won't hurt as much.

Now, can you put his arm in the sling? That will help with the pain too!

Great! One last thing, the ice packs! Can you put those in the sling? That should help keep the swelling down.

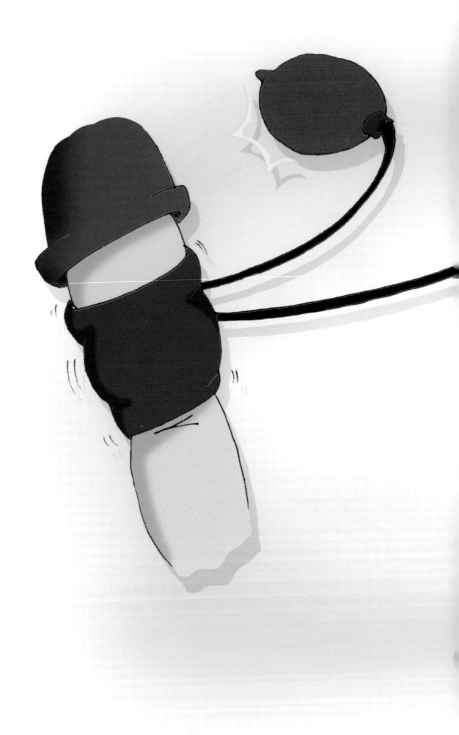

We need to take some vital signs. Why don't you take
his blood pressure and check his pulse rate.

Can you put the blood pressure cuff in the right place?

Can you show me where you take a pulse?

Perfect heart rate and blood pressure!

Here we are at hospital. The doctors and nurses will want to hear what happened, and what we did. Can you tell them about the accident and how we helped Tommie?

So, what did we learn today? You should always wear your safety gear, because you never know when you might have an accident. Safety first!

Great job today, partner. I can't wait to work with you again. I will see you the next time someone needs our help!

About the Authors

The authors are real paramedics! Chris and Nicole have over twenty years of combined experience in Emergency Medical Services. They want to pass on their experiences in a way that children will discover what to expect if they ever find themselves or others in need of Emergency Medical Services.

Frederick the Paramedic is designed to engage the reader as Frederick's partner on an ambulance. Together, Frederick and your child will check out the equipment that is stocked in a real ambulance. They will assess a patient, and determine what interventions are appropriate for that particular situation. Once the patient arrives at the hospital, your Junior Paramedic will give a report to the doctors and nurses in the Emergency Room, recalling the incident and any interventions they provided.

Visit us at
fredericktheparamedic.com